To the two KCs

www.mascotbooks.com

I Walked My Dog Around the Pond

For more information, please contact:
Mascot Books
560 Herndon Parkway #120
Herndon, VA 20170
info@mascotbooks.com

Library of Congress Control Number: 2017940484

CPSIA Code: PBANG0517A
ISBN-13: 978-1-68401-136-0

Printed in the United States

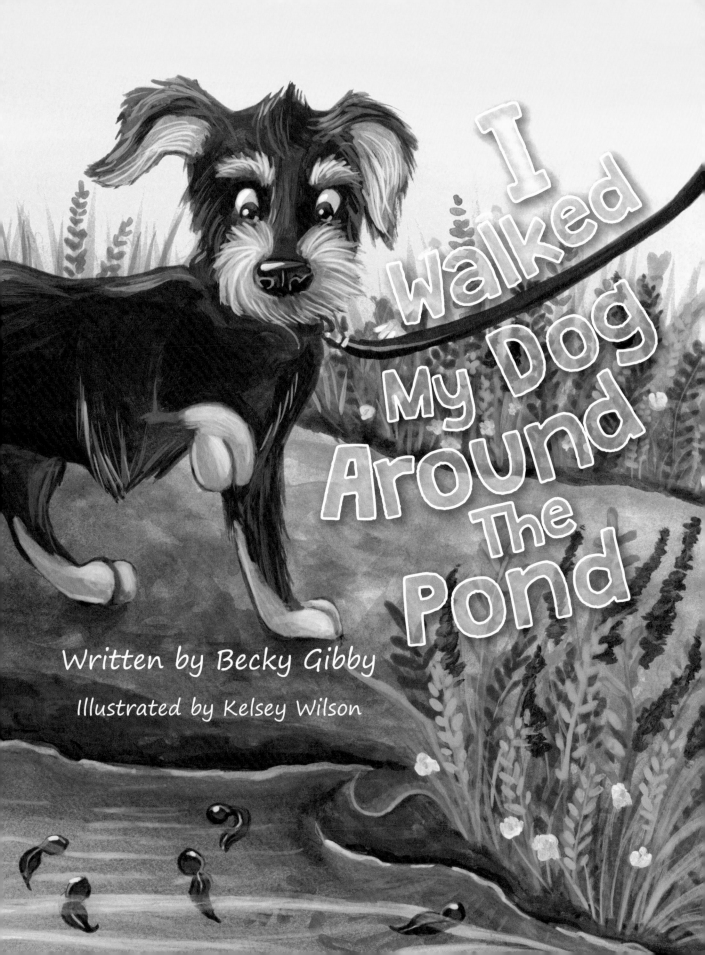

January

I walked my dog around the pond
In the **January** chill.
One Blue Heron flew overhead,
A minnow in his bill.

1

February

I walked my dog around the pond.
February winds stung my cheeks.
Two groundhogs popped up,
Then went back to sleep a few more weeks.

2

March

I walked my dog around the pond
In **March's** sleet and snow.
Three Mallard ducks were swimming laps
And diving down below.

April

I walked my dog around the pond.
April rains puddled at my feet.
Four fat robins hopped in the mud
Searching for worms to eat.

May

I walked my dog around the pond.
May brought a soft, sweet breeze.
Five squiggly tadpoles swam in the sun
And waved their tails with ease.

(5)

June

I walked my dog around the pond.
June grew warm and bright.
Six croaking frogs sang all day
And long into the night.

6

July

I walked my dog around the pond,
As **July** got hot and dry.
Seven trout with speckled fins
Jumped up to catch a fly.

August

I walked my dog around the pond.
August afternoons grew cool.
Eight shy deer came down to drink
From the clear, delicious pool.

September

I walked my dog around the pond,
While September storms blew by.
Nine gray squirrels foraged for nuts
To store in their nests up high.

9

October

I walked my dog around the pond.
October days made me shiver.
Ten wild turkeys pushed through dead leaves,
Their tail feathers all aquiver.

10

November

I walked my dog around the pond.
November winds whipped the waves.
Eleven gray geese went for a dip
And honked, "Don't you think we're brave?"

11

December

I walked my dog around the pond.
December turned water to glass.
Twelve red cardinals called to the world,
"Cheeeeeeer! Cheer for the year that passed!"

12

About the Author

Born and raised in Philadelphia, Becky Gibby honed her writing skills by working on children's drama and primary song lyrics. She holds a Bachelor's Degree in elementary education from the University of Pennsylvania and a Master's Degree from Drew University. Becky lives in Chatham, New Jersey. The pond in this story is Kelley's Pond (formerly Milton Pond behind Milton Avenue School) where she walked her children and years later her dog, KC. This book is an homage to Chatham, a wonderful place to raise a family.

Have a book idea?

Contact us at:

info@mascotbooks.com | www.mascotbooks.com